LADYBIRD BOOKS

UK | USA | Canada | Ireland | Australia
India | New Zealand | South Africa
Ladybird Books is part of the Penguin Random House group of companies
whose addresses can be found at global.penguinrandomhouse.com.

www.penguin.co.uk   www.puffin.co.uk   www.ladybird.co.uk

First published 2014 as part of the Ladybird First Favourite Tales series
This Ladybird Picture Books edition published 2017
003

Printed in China
A CIP catalogue record for this book is available from the British Library

ISBN: 978–0–241–31540–8

All correspondence to:
Ladybird Books, Penguin Random House Children's
80 Strand, London WC2R 0RL

Ladybird Picture Books

The Ugly Duckling

BASED ON A TALE BY HANS CHRISTIAN ANDERSEN
retold by Mandy Ross ★ illustrated by Ailie Busby

Once upon a springtime, a mother duck was sitting on six smooth eggs.

One day, with a *creak* and a *crack*, out hatched five fluffy, feathery little ducklings.

There was just one egg left in the nest and it was much BIGGER than all the rest.

At last, with a *creak* and a *crack*, the big
egg hatched. Out popped a big, raggedy
grey duckling. He wasn't like the others.
What an ugly duckling!

Hello!

"You're different to us, but I won't make a fuss!" quacked Mother Duck. "You're still one of my babies."

Mother Duck and all her ducklings came to the water. *Splish! Splash!* They all went in for a swim.

The little yellow ducklings splashed and quacked.
But the ugly duckling paddled quietly at the back.

Mother Duck and her ducklings came into the busy duckyard.

The other ducks gathered round.
"Look at them all! What pretty darlings!
Except this one."

Mother Duck tucked the ugly duckling
under her wing.

The ducks in the duckyard didn't like the ugly duckling.
"*Quack, quack, QUACK! Don't come back!*" they quacked.

Even Mother Duck couldn't protect him.

So the ugly duckling ran away.
He searched for somewhere safe to stay.

The ugly duckling came to a marsh where wild ducks swam. But...

"What an ugly duckling!" quacked the wild ducks. "*Quack, quack, QUACK! Don't come back!*"

So the ugly duckling swam away.
He searched for somewhere safe to stay.

The ugly duckling came to a cosy old cottage.
But...

"Can you *purrrrrr*, like me?" purred the cat.
"*Cluck! Cluck!* And can you lay eggs, like me?"
clucked the hen.
"No," said the ugly duckling sadly.
"*Cluck! Cluck! CLUCK!* Don't come back!"
said the hen.

So the ugly duckling ran away.
He searched for somewhere safe to stay.

At last the ugly duckling came to a quiet lake. "There's nobody here to chase me away. This is somewhere safe to stay," he thought.

One evening, high up in the sky, the ugly
duckling saw a flock of white swans flying by.
"I wish I could join them," he thought sadly.

All through the winter, the ugly duckling lived alone on the quiet lake.

The days grew colder and colder. Snow fell and the lake froze to ice.

One frozen morning, a farmer found the ugly duckling shivering and quivering with cold. He brought him inside to warm him up.

He said, "Look who I've found." But the children just chased him around and around.

The ugly duckling ran away. He ran back to the quiet lake, where it was safe to stay.

The winter was long and very cold.
The ugly duckling wished, "If only..."

At last, spring came. The warm sun shone.
Soon the snow and ice were gone.
The flock of swans flew by, high up in the sky.

The ugly duckling thought, "I don't want to
be lonely any longer." He spread his wings.
He was bigger... and stronger.

The swans flew down to the lake. They greeted the ugly duckling, one by one. "Pleased to meet such a fine young swan!" In the water, the ugly duckling suddenly caught a glimpse of himself.

His ugly grey feathers had gone.
He gasped, "I'm a beautiful swan!"
"Join us!" called the swans. And so he did.

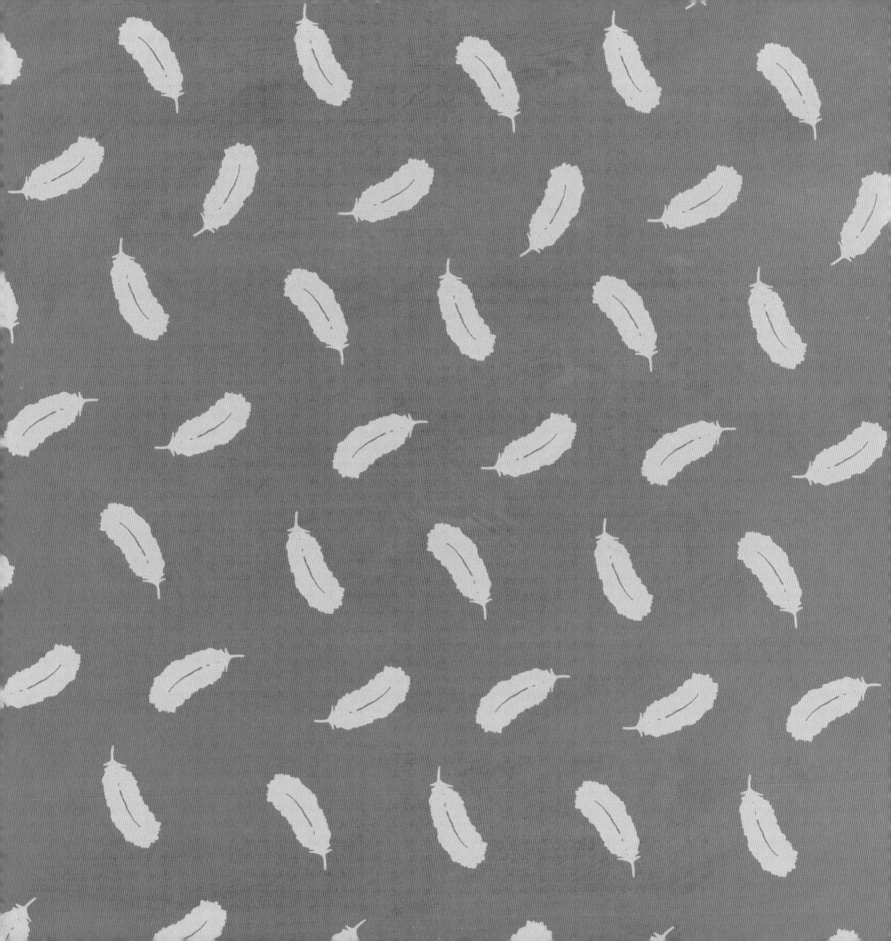

Ladybird Picture Books

Look out for...

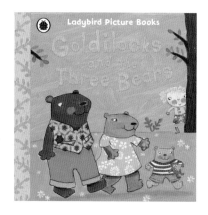

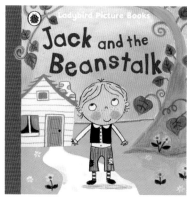

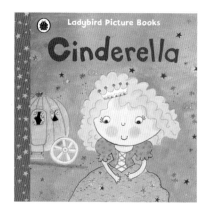

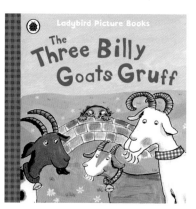

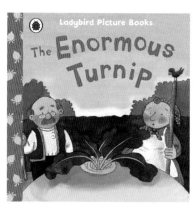

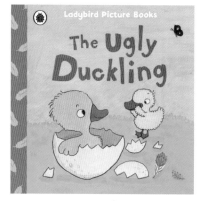

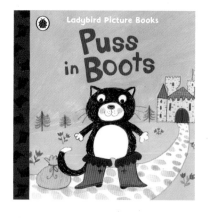

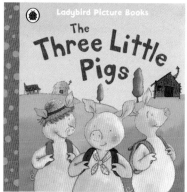